Heads Up, Horses!

A KONA STORY

By Sibley Miller

Illustrated by Tara Larsen Chang and Jo Gershman

Feiwel and Friends

For Mia, Ben, and Naomi—Sibley Miller

To Susan Summit Cyr for her knowledge of horses
and her artistic skills, both shared with generosity
—Tara Larsen Chang and Jo Gershman

A FEIWEL AND FRIENDS BOOK
An Imprint of Macmillan

Library of Congress Cataloging-in-Publication Data Available

ISBN: 978-0-312-56220-5

DESIGNED BY BARBARA GRZESLO
Feiwel and Friends logo designed by Filomena Tuosto

First Edition: 2009

1 3 5 7 9 10 8 6 4 2

www.feiwelandfriends.com

CONTENTS

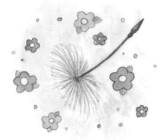

Meet the Wind Dancers

One day, a lonely little girl named Leanna blows on a doozy of a dandelion. To her delight and surprise, four tiny horses spring from the puff of the dandelion seeds!

Four tiny horses with shiny manes and shimmery wings. Four magical horses who can fly!

Dancing on the wind, surrounded by magic halos, they are the Wind Dancers.

The leader of the quartet is **Kona**. She has a violet-black coat and vivid purple mane, and she flies inside a halo of magical flowers.

Brisa is as pretty as a tropical sunset with her coral-pink color and blonde mane and tail.

Magical jewels make up Brisa's halo, and she likes to admire her gems (and herself) every time she looks in a mirror.

Sumatra is silvery blue with sea-green wings. Much like the ocean, she can shift from calm to stormy in a hurry! Her magical halo is made up of ribbons, which flutter and dance as she flies.

The fourth Wind Dancer is—surprise!—a colt. His name is Sirocco. He's a fiery gold, and he likes to go-go-go. Everywhere he goes, his magical halo of butterflies goes, too.

The tiny, flying horses live together in the dandelion meadow in a lovely house carved out of the trunk of an apple tree. Every day, Leanna wishes she'll see the magical little horses again. (She's sure they're nearby, but she doesn't know they're invisible to people.) And the Wind Dancers get ready for their next adventure.

CHAPTER 1
Kick Off!

It was a bright day in the dandelion meadow, but as she flew with Brisa, Sumatra, and Sirocco, Kona was feeling as blue as the sky.

"I don't know *what* we should do today," she said with a sigh. She flew over to a branch of an oak tree and kicked an acorn. It sailed through the air and landed with a *plunk* in an abandoned bird's nest in a neighboring tree.

"Looks to me like you're doing something already!" Sumatra said, impressed.

"What do you mean?" Kona asked dully.

"Hello? You just made a nest in one!"

Sirocco pointed out. He kicked at the air, only to send himself into a wobbly double backflip. "Whoa!"

"As you can see," Sumatra said dryly, as the Wind Dancers flew on, "not everyone has your kicking talent, Kona."

"That's why you were such a star in Sumatra's talent show!" Brisa added sweetly.

"That's nice of you to say," Kona said, sighing again, "but lately, my kicking has kind of . . . lost its kick for me."

The horses had arrived at the school, which was surrounded by a tall, wooden fence. Idly, Kona reached out and tapped a hoof against a pinecone dangling from a nearby tree branch. The cone landed in a knot in the fence and stuck fast!

Sirocco gaped at Kona's bull's-eye.

"You're such a kicker!" he sputtered.

Kona tried to smile at Sirocco, but she feared it came out as more of a frown.

"Here's the thing," Kona said to her friends. "Sumatra's talent show is so last month. Now, I've got nobody to entertain with my kicking!"

"But that doesn't mean you have to stop practicing," Sumatra said encouragingly to Kona. "With every kick, you're getting better and better at hitting targets!"

"But I think I've kicked every acorn, pinecone, and apple in this meadow," Kona answered. She swooped down and kicked up a stone on the ground with her hoof. Then she rose back into the air, casually juggling the stone from hoof to hoof. "And I've kicked them at every tree knot, branch, and bird's nest I could possibly find."

"You're weird!" Sirocco said. "Can you imagine me saying, 'Oh, I've eaten every kind of pie ever invented, so I'll just stop now?'"

Before Kona could respond, she heard a high-pitched voice on the other side of the fence.

"Over here! Kick it!"

"What?" Kona exclaimed. She was so stunned, she fumbled and dropped her stone.

"You guys!" Kona said to her friends, breathlessly. "Did you hear that? It sounded like a girl. A girl wanting me to kick my stone to her!"

"But how is that possible?" Sumatra gasped. "People can't see us!"

"Or . . . can they?" Kona said excitedly. "Maybe things have changed."

Together, the Wind Dancers flew nearer to the fence to get a closer look. As they fluttered in the air, they spotted the girl who'd called out to Kona.

And she was—guess who?—Leanna!

Her brown eyes sparkled, and her wavy, blonde hair bounced in a sporty ponytail.

The Wind Dancers were too thrilled and excited to speak. Finally, Leanna was able to see them!

Kona held her breath and waited for Leanna to say hello.

Leanna looked straight at Kona and she shouted again.

"I've got it, I've got it!" she called.

"I'm confused," Kona said to her friends. "What does Leanna mean—"

"Look out!" Sumatra interrupted her.

Kona followed Sumatra's gaze and neighed in alarm. Then she darted to the side just in time to avoid being beaned by a giant black-and-white ball!

Kona watched as Leanna skillfully fielded the ball, not with her hands but with her foot! She kicked it to a girl who was running toward her. The girl, in turn, kicked it toward a large, rectangular net. An identical net rested at the opposite end of the field.

Kona was so fascinated by this game that she almost forgot to be disappointed that Leanna, as always, couldn't see them.

Until she looked at Sumatra, Sirocco, and Brisa.

"Leanna wasn't talking to us!" Sumatra said with a wail.

"We're still invisible to people," Sirocco agreed glumly.

"No matter how beautiful we are," Brisa added, with a sigh.

Searching desperately for something that would cheer up her friends, Kona pointed her hoof down at the playing field.

"Isn't that the most amazing game?"

The other Wind Dancers glanced at the running, shouting, kicking kids.

"They're using their feet to catch that big ball," Sumatra said, bewildered.

"Or their heads!" Sirocco exclaimed, as

one of the girls bounced the black-and-white ball off her forehead.

"They look like they're having such fun," Brisa added.

Kona's eyes drifted back to the game. Leanna had the black-and-white ball again. She was dribbling it down the field. Half of the girls seemed to be chasing her, while the other half were protecting her from the ones who were chasing her!

Kona caught her breath as Leanna forged ahead and punted the ball into the net.

"Goal!" Leanna shouted, throwing her hands above her head. A few of her teammates gathered around her and cheered, while the kids on the other team kicked at the dirt in frustration.

From the sidelines, a teacher shouted, "Good play, Leanna! The score's one to zero!"

"Wow!" Kona breathed, turning back to her friends. "Blocking goals. And scoring goals. And gaining points. This game takes kicking to a whole new level!"

"I wonder what it's called," Sirocco said.

"Wait here!" Kona told her friends. She zipped down to the playing field.

Kona quickly figured out that each team

wanted to kick the ball into the other team's net. But it wasn't as simple as that. There were lots of rules. You couldn't foul (that means touch) another player to get the ball away from her, and you couldn't go outside

the lines of thc playing field.

Kona watched it all intensely.

And that's how she learned the name of this wonderful game.

When Kona finally flew up to rejoin the other Wind Dancers, her black eyes were gleaming and her purple tail was arched high in the air.

"The game," she announced dramatically, "is called 'soccer.' And I can't *wait* to play it!"

CHAPTER 2
Paddock of Dreams

Kona waited for her friends to whinny in excitement. But instead, Brisa had an announcement of her own!

"I know what that game reminds me of," she cried. "Andy!"

"Andy?" Kona said. "You mean Thelma's new foal?"

Thelma was one of the giant, non-flying, un-magical horses the Wind Dancers had met on their very first day in

the dandelion meadow.
The chestnut mare
lived in a paddock
with two friends—
Benny, a haughty black
gelding, and Fluff, a little filly with a dappled
gray coat. Now that Thelma
had a baby colt, Andy, the
big horses were a crew
of four.

Unlike the Wind
Dancers, the big horses had
human owners, who brushed them and fed
them and took them out for rides. And they
weren't, of course, invisible to people the way
the Wind Dancers were.

The Wind Dancers thought it was all a
bit strange.

The big horses thought the Wind Dancers
were a bit strange, too.

But, the Wind Dancers and the big horses were all, well, horses. And they all lived in the same dandelion meadow. So, they were friends. Especially since baby Andy had arrived—and Brisa had fallen head over hooves for him.

"Why don't we go visit?" Brisa proposed with a grin. "Unlike people, Andy can see us. And he's sooooo cute!"

"Here Brisa goes again," Sumatra giggled.

"I love his little knock-knees," Brisa said with a happy sigh. "And the way his forelock flops into his eyes. And—"

"—and what about soccer?" Kona interrupted Brisa eagerly. "Don't you think it would be so much fun to play?"

"I don't know," Brisa crooned. "That black-and-white ball isn't nearly as cute as baby Annnnndy."

Kona felt a little desperate. How could she get the Wind Dancers to play soccer if Brisa was so busy cooing over Thelma's little colt?!

"Brisa," Kona cautioned, "I don't know if Thelma's going to want us hanging around Andy. You know how tough she can be!"

"Oh, please!" Brisa scoffed, her eyes still dreamy. "A mommy just loves it when other horses fuss over her cute little baaaaby!"

"He *is* adorable," Sumatra admitted.

"I wonder if he's old enough to talk about guy stuff," Sirocco chimed in.

"Okay, okay," Kona grumbled. "Let's go visit the big horses."

The Wind Dancers fluttered in the air and headed for the big horses' paddock.

"You know what's neat about soccer?" Kona said as they flew. "It's just like kicking, but better! Because it's got other players. Teams! Isn't that great?"

"Sure, I guess," Sumatra said as she flapped her green wings evenly. "I don't get the point, though. Why does one team want to score goals against the other?"

Kona gaped at Sumatra.

"Hello?" she exclaimed. "To win!"

"Well, what do you win?" asked Sirocco. "A pie? If there's food, I'll sign up for soccer!"

"You don't win something," Kona said with a frown. "At least, I don't think so. The point is just to know that you're the *best*!"

"Uh-huh," Sumatra yawned.

"When you think about it," Kona pressed on slyly, "a game where you don't use your hands is perfect for us. We've got nothing but feet! In fact, I think we'd be soccer stars. After we visit Andy, why don't we divide up into teams of two and play soccer against each other!"

Sumatra stopped yawning and neighed in alarm!

"*Divide* up?" she said. "Play *against* each other? Kona, 'divide' and 'against' aren't very Wind Dancery words. The four of us are a team. You don't want to break us up, do you?"

Kona snorted dismissively.

"Oh, Sumatra," she said. "It's just a fun game. Don't you want to play? And win?"

"Well, I'm not sure," Sumatra countered. "If it's just a game, winning shouldn't be important, right?"

"No, you don't get it!" Kona insisted, shaking her head. "Winning is what makes playing a game fun!"

Sumatra just looked at her blankly.

Sirocco did another loop-de-loop.

And Brisa zipped ahead, singing, "La, la, la! I can't wait to play with the baaaaaby!"

"Fine," Kona said with a frown. "I guess soccer is just a game I *won't* get to play."

. . .

"Wheeeee!"

Andy whinnied playfully from the big horses' paddock when he saw the Wind Dancers approaching. He hopped up on his hind legs, pawing at the air.

"Oh, Andy," Kona said with a laugh, as she fluttered up to the colt. "You can't fly!"

"But you're adorable, anyway," Brisa quickly assured the foal, stroking his silky ears with her nose. "Even without wings."

Thelma trotted up, her nostrils flaring!

"Even without wings?!" she repeated indignantly. She turned to her little colt.

"Andy, trust me, you don't want wings," Thelma told him. "Galloping on the ground is much more dignified than whizzing through the air like tiny horseflies. Using your hooves is just more . . . horsey. You'll understand when you're older."

"Well, I'm older and I still don't understand," said a quiet, raspy voice from behind Thelma. All the horses turned and saw Fluff, the dappled gray filly.

"I wish I could fly, too!" Fluff added with a shy smile.

Thelma rolled her eyes and neighed over to the last of the big horses, the gelding, who was on the other side of the paddock, pointedly ignoring the group.

"Benny," she called. "Will you talk some sense into Fluff? She's filling Andy's head with silly Wind Dancer dreams."

The Wind Dancers looked at each other and rolled their eyes, too.

Oh, Thelma! Kona thought with a smug grin. *She doesn't understand how amazing*

it is to be magic.

Then her smile dimmed as she added to herself, *Just like Sirocco, Sumatra, and Brisa don't understand how magical it can be to play soccer!*

Meanwhile, Benny trotted up. He tossed his black mane proudly.

"Ah, Fluff," he scoffed. "Why would you want to be a puny little Wind Dancer when you're a big, beautiful horse?!"

"Maybe because we have magic halos, for one!" Sumatra suggested.

"And we're beautiful!" Brisa added, spinning so her magic jewels sparkled in the sunshine.

"And . . . and . . . we know about a sport called soccer!" Kona burst out.

Benny snorted. "Whatever—hey, wait a minute, what was that last one?"

For the first time since the Wind Dancers had arrived, Benny looked at them with more than a little interest.

Kona felt a glimmer of hope. Benny was always looking for a way to prove that the big horses were better than the little Wind Dancers. Maybe she could get him to agree to play soccer! (And by the time he realized Kona was a champion kicker, it would be too late!)

"Soccer," Kona explained, "is the *best* game ever!"

"Hmmm," Benny said thoughtfully. He sounded intrigued.

"You see," Kona went on excitedly, "you make a line down the center of the field. Each team starts on opposite sides of the line. But once you kick off, you can run anywhere you want! Then you use your hooves or your head to pass a ball to your teammates and try to score goals!"

As Kona continued to explain soccer to Benny, the bouncy foal began to play with a big, red Jolly Ball.

"See?" Kona said with a grin. "Andy is showing us his toy ball! *He* gets it! The only other things you need to get a soccer game started are two goals."

Excitedly, Kona flew to one end of the oval paddock. There was a nearly empty water trough next to the fence.

"One goal," she announced, pointing to the trough with her nose. On the other side of the

paddock was a hay manger. She winged over to it and declared, "Two goals!"

"But Kona," Sumatra protested, sounding hurt, "remember what we said about dividing and conquering before?"

"I do remember," Kona replied, her eyes gleaming. "But I've just realized how we can play soccer and still be a team. We can play against the big horses!"

Sumatra's mouth dropped open. Brisa's wide, sparkly eyes got wider and even more sparkly. And Sirocco did a back-flip in the

air (which Andy, clumsily, tried to imitate).

"I guess I can't argue with that," Sumatra admitted.

"Four against four!" Sirocco declared. "That's perfect!"

Then he looked at Benny and Thelma and

said, "That is, if you big horses are up for the challenge!"

"Oh," Thelma began haughtily, "I don't *think* so—"

But Benny cut her off with a competitive neigh.

"We are *so* ready," he neighed at Sirocco. He pawed at the dirt with his hoof while Andy kicked at the Jolly Ball with a giggly whinny.

Eyeing her happy foal, Thelma rolled her eyes once more.

"Oh, well," she blustered. "If Andy wants to play this silly game, I suppose I'll go along with it. For now."

"Hooray!" Kona cried. Grinning, she flew over to Brisa.

"Like you said, Brisa, moms can't resist it when their babies want something!" she whispered.

"Especially when their babies are as cute as Annnnndy," Brisa replied.

"Uh-huh," Kona said absentmindedly. "The important thing is, now we get to play soccer! This is my first victory of the day!"

Brisa frowned in confusion.

"Victory?" she said. "I don't get it. Is the point of this whole soccer thing to play or to win?"

"Do you even have to ask?" Kona whinnied. "Both!"

She began doing practice kicks in the air with all four legs.

"OKAY, EVERYONE," she shouted, "LET'S PLAY BALL!"

CHAPTER 3

A Mismatched (Soccer) Match

The big horses tipped over the water trough and hay manger to make them into goals, while Brisa and Sirocco dragged a stick across the paddock to draw their "soccer field's" center line. Then Kona clopped her front hooves together.

"Perfect!" she said. "There's only one thing missing."

"What's that?" Sumatra asked, perplexed.

"Well," Kona responded, "Leanna and her friends had a grown-up working with them. Someone who knew all the rules and kept score. You know—a referee."

"Okay," Benny said with a shrug. "So we need a referee."

"But who should it be?" Kona said, forcing her face into an innocent expression. "Are any of you interested?"

Sirocco snorted.

"Oh, *please*," he said, waving a hoof at Kona. "We all know you're going to be the referee. You know the rules of the game the best. And you want to be the referee the most. And besides, you're too bossy *not* to be the referee."

"I'm not bossy!" Kona protested.

She saw the big and little horses exchange glances and suppress giggles. Well, except for Thelma—who laughed right out loud.

Kona decided to ignore this slight. She didn't want to give Thelma any reason to call off the game. Instead, she said primly, "Well, it *is* true that I paid the most attention to Leanna's soccer game. So, Sirocco, if you were nominating me to be referee, I accept."

Kona smiled at both teams generously.

This time, they all laughed out loud. But Benny also plodded to their soccer field's center line and said, "Okay, referee, tell me which side of the field belongs to the Bigs 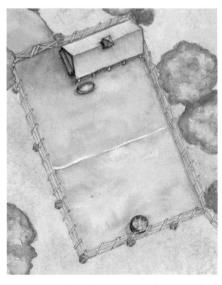 and we can get this show on the road."

"Um, that one!" Kona said, as she pointed to the south side of the paddock. "The hay manger is your goal and the water trough is ours. Now let's flip a coin to see who gets the first kick. . . ."

"We're horses," Thelma interrupted. "We don't have any money, nor do we have thumbs for flipping."

"Oh . . . you're right," Kona responded, feeling embarrassed.

"Oh, forget it," Benny huffed. "You Wind Dancers can have the kickoff. What does it matter anyway?"

"What does it matter?!" Kona sputtered. "The team with the kickoff gets to charge for the goal first! The other team can only defend itself. Our team would have a very good chance of scoring the first goal!"

"We'll see about that!" Benny taunted.

Kona trembled with excitement as she lined herself up behind the ball.

The big horses asked for this, she thought. *I just hope they're not too upset when the Wind Dancer team makes the first goal!*

Kona gave the ball the mightiest kick she

had! It sailed up into the air and landed smack dab— on Fluff's hoof!

"Ooh!" Fluff said in surprise. The ball bounced off her hoof and flew in the opposite direction!

The ball went so high and so fast and so far that it left the Wind Dancers in its dust! All they could do was chase it as it flew— straight into the water trough!

The big horses gaped as the ball bounced around the trough. Finally, Fluff stammered, "I . . . I scored!"

"Goooooooaaaaaaalllll!" Benny neighed, rearing back on his hind legs.

Thelma looked at Kona.

"That makes the score one-zippo," she

said with a grin. "I hope you're not too upset that we made the first goal."

Kona was grateful for the violet-black hair that hid the flush in her face.

"Upset?" she scoffed. "Not at all."

In her head she added, *I'm not upset. Oh, no—I'm too enraged, baffled, and embarrassed to be UPSET!*

But now the Wind Dancers had the ball again. Sirocco kicked it to Sumatra, but Thelma knocked the ball away from the little Wind Dancer with one casual tap of her giant hoof.

"Hey!" Sumatra complained.

Whinnying, Kona dove for the ball, but before she could make her kick, Benny nudged her out of the way with his enormous nose! He bopped the ball with his knee. The next thing Kona knew—

"Goooooooaaaaaaalllll!"

This time it was Fluff who yelled out in

triumph as the ball plopped neatly into the water trough.

"Whoops!" Brisa said with a giggle. "I think Benny, Fluff, and Thelma are outbigging us!"

Kona glowered.

"They may be big, but we're tall," Kona muttered to her teammates.

Sumatra and Sirocco glanced at each other—in all their four-inch-tall glory.

"Um, how do you figure that?" Sumatra wondered.

"Like this!" Kona declared. Kicking the ball out of the water trough, she juggled it from her knee to her head to her hoof, keeping the ball aloft. As she dribbled the ball, she flew up, up, up in the air.

She was so high up that Thelma couldn't reach the ball even when she reared up on her hind legs!

"S-i-r-o-c-c-o!" Kona shouted, as she got

ready to pass the ball
to the colt. Sirocco
zipped upward to
field it.

"Hey!" Benny
complained, while
Andy again tried
to launch himself
into the air. "Get
down here!"

"Sure!" Kona agreed
as Sirocco passed the ball
back to her. "I just have to do *one* thing first."

With that, she head-butted the ball out of
the sky—and straight into the big horses' hay-
manger goal!

"Whoo, hooooooo!" Kona celebrated.

Until three voices cried out, "No fair!"

Those voices belonged to Thelma,
Benny—and Brisa!

"Brisa!" Kona said in shock. "What's not fair about helping our team win?"

"Well, the big horses can't fly," Brisa said sweetly. "It just doesn't seem sporting to play from way up in the air."

"But they're so much bigger than us—you said it yourself," Kona blustered. "That's not fair either, is it?"

"You're right," Fluff chimed in. "We're too big for you to beat, and you're too high-flying for us to beat."

"Unless—" Kona began.

"Unless what?" Sumatra asked.

"Unless we evened things up by mixing them up," Kona replied. "Two big horses and two Wind Dancers to a team."

"Ooh, yes!" Fluff cried. "I get to play on a Wind Dancers team!"

"As referee, I'll choose the teams," Kona said bossily. "On my team, I'll take Sirocco, Benny, and Thelma."

As in, the fastest horse (Sirocco), the strongest horse (Benny), and the most stubborn horse (Thelma)! Kona thought, trying to conceal her smug smile.

"I don't *think* so!" Thelma protested. "Nobody's putting me on a different team from my foal!"

B-but . . . Kona thought, *Andy can't even say soccer, much less play it! With a wobbly little foal on my team, I'll never win!*

But, as Thelma licked Andy's nose and Brisa tickled his ears, Kona knew she couldn't say this out loud.

"Okay, fine!" she huffed. "My team will have Sirocco, Thelma, and Andy. Brisa, Sumatra, Benny, and Fluff can play on the other team."

"Done," Thelma agreed.

Andy bucked and whinnied in delight.

Sumatra wasn't as happy.

"So you're really doing it?" Sumatra asked sadly. "You're breaking up the Wind Dancers' team? Our family?!"

Kona felt a twinge of guilt. But one glance at the red ball still in the hay manger after her

triumphant goal brushed that feeling away.

"C'mon, filly," she responded scoffily to Sumatra. "Remember, this is just a game! Just because we're splitting up here doesn't mean we're not a team everywhere else."

"Not everything's a competition, Kona," Sumatra said, as her magic-ribbon halo drooped.

"But this game is!" Kona said, her eyes going bright as she eyed the red ball again. "Don't you want to get going?"

Sunatra looked at Brisa and Sirocco, and rolled her eyes.

"There's no stopping her," she whispered. "I guess the only thing we can do—"

"—is play ball on our new teams!" Brisa finished.

CHAPTER 4
A Rigorous Referee

T weet, tweet, tweeeeet!

When that shrill noise sounded almost halfway through the new game, Benny stumbled over the pass he'd just received. He tripped so hard, in fact, that one of the bell boots he was wearing (to protect himself during play) flew off! The gelding spun and stared at Kona, who was holding a blade of grass between her lips and blowing through it with all her might.

"Why are you blowing that horrible thing?!" Benny bellowed.

"You're offsides," Kona said primly.

"Off what?" Benny asked incredulously. "What does that mean?"

"When a pass is made to you," Kona explained, "you can't be closer to the goal than any of our players."

"But," Fluff said simply, "we didn't know that, Kona."

"It's a basic rule of soccer!" Kona said. "*Everybody* knows that!"

"And we would have, too," Sumatra said with a glower, "if you had just told us—"

Tweeet!

"My team gets a free kick," Kona said sweetly. "I'll take it."

Before Benny could say, "What's a free kick?!" Kona had swooped down, grabbed the ball, placed it at a sweet spot right near the hay manger, and kicked it before any of the other players could react.

"Gooooaaaaaalllll!" Kona shouted, flying a triumphant lap around the paddock. "My third one of the game! Too bad you guys have only scored once!"

"Hello, up there!" Benny called irritably. "Do you want to play or do you want to stage a victory parade?"

"Oh, calm down, it's just a game," Kona said, giggling triumphantly. She flew down to the field so Benny's team could kick off. But no sooner had Brisa passed the ball to Fluff than—

Tweeeet!

"What now?" Brisa demanded.

"Out of bounds," Kona said, pointing at Fluff, who'd been dribbling the ball near the paddock fence.

"What bounds?" Fluff said, looking around in confusion.

"There are boundaries behind the goals and along the sides," Kona said, a bit smugly. "Once you've touched the fence, you're out of bounds."

"But, but—"

Tweeeeet!

"You're still out of bounds," Kona said.

Kona took a deep breath and tweeted some more—until Andy trotted up, plucked the grass blade from between Kona's lips, and ate it!

All the horses—except Kona—burst out laughing.

49

"That's the best call all day," Thelma said, giving Andy a nose nuzzle while he nipped playfully at the pretty blue workout wraps warming her forelegs.

Trying to maintain her dignity, Kona declared, "Clearly, some players are hungry. As referee, I say it's—lunchtime! But remember, we've still got a half game left. And let's also not forget that the score is three to one!"

"Oh, I'm sure you won't forget," Sumatra sniped, as the tiny horses flew and the big ones trotted to a shady part of the paddock. "After all, your team is winning."

"Cheer up," Sirocco said to Sumatra. "Why care about losing a game when you're gaining food?"

"I'll pretend I didn't hear that," Kona said as she unwrapped the picnic lunch that she'd prepared that morning. While the big horses munched on hay nearby, Kona doled out food to the Wind Dancers.

"Wow, Kona," Sirocco said as he dug into his lunch. "This is awesome! Honey on oatmeal bread, apple fritters, and carrot pudding!"

"Enjoy," Kona said breezily, taking her own bite of carrot pudding.

That's when Brisa nudged Sumatra.

"That's funny," she said, frowning at her own food. "I think Kona forgot to give me carrot pudding. And look, I've only got a slice of bread—no honey. And did Sirocco say apple fritters? I didn't get any apple fritters."

"Me neither!" Sumatra said, gaping at her own paltry picnic.

"Kona must have made a mistake," Brisa said sweetly. She turned to the violet horse and said, "Oh, Kon—"

But just then, Kona used her nose to roll another apple fritter over to Sirocco.

"Eat up!" she told him. "You need your strength to help us win the game!"

Brisa and Sumatra gaped at each other.

"It wasn't a mistake," Brisa whispered.

"She's trying to starve us so we'll lose the soccer game!" Sumatra whispered back.

Sumatra turned to Kona, her nostrils flaring, but before she could say anything, Kona was swallowing her last bite and fluttering into the air.

"I think I'll go give Andy some coaching," she said to Sirocco. "The little guy doesn't know a corner kick from a throw-in!"

As Kona flew off, Brisa said to Sumatra, "Kona knows all the rules. And she gets all the best food. And she gets extra cuddle time with cute little Andy! This is no fair!"

"You're right!" Sirocco agreed unhappily, between big bites of apple fritter.

"What are you complaining about?" Sumatra asked bitterly. "You've had *more* than enough to eat!"

"Yeah," Sirocco said. "But Kona used to give me warm fuzzies, too."

"She was like a mom to all of us," Brisa agreed. "Until the game got to her."

"Guess what?" Sumatra announced suddenly to Brisa and Sirocco. "Kona's not the only one with tricks up her wings!"

"What do you mean?" Brisa asked.

"Wait and see," Sumatra whispered with a grin. Then she zipped out of the paddock.

When Sumatra returned a while later, she wasn't alone. Huffing and puffing along the ground beneath her was a roly-poly squirrel with a kind, buck-toothed grin!

"Gray!" Kona, Sirocco, and Brisa cried.

Gray was the nice squirrel who'd given the Wind Dancers their carved-out apple tree house on their first day in the dandelion meadow.

"Did you come to watch a victory?" Kona asked the squirrel proudly.

"Actually," Gray replied, "I'm your new referee!"

"Referee?!" Kona gasped. "But . . . but *I'm* the referee!"

"And you must be tired!" Sumatra said, innocently blinking her long green lashes at Kona. "It's awfully hard to play soccer and call the shots at the same time. It's so hard, in fact, that you only seem to see the mistakes our team makes. And never the ones on your side of the soccer field!"

Kona blushed.

"Oh, fine!" she blurted. "The squirrel stays. Let's just get started on the second half, already."

"Okay, horses," Gray said with a grin, "the score stands at three to one. I want a clean game. No tail-swatting, no kicking—"

"But Gray," Kona protested, "it's soccer!"

"Oh," Gray said, blinking. "So kicking's okay, then?"

"How can you referee," Kona complained, "if you don't even know how to play the game?"

"Ah, don't worry about it!" Gray said, thumping his chest proudly with both paws. "I'll pick it up as I go. Besides, Sumatra told me there's a thing you say about soccer: 'It's just a game.' Right?"

"It's just a game with very specific rules," Kona grumbled. She flew to join her teammates, positioning herself just beside Andy's flip-floppy left ear.

"Just remember all the coaching I gave you during lunch," she whispered to the foal. "Always pass the ball to me, and we'll do great!"

Andy reared back on his hind legs, flicking playfully at Kona with his front hooves.

"Right! That's what you need to do—kick to me!" Kona cried, thinking herself a very talented coach. "You've got it!"

"The only thing that colt's got," Benny teased from the other side of the field, "is the urge to fly."

"We'll show you," Kona retorted.

"Alright," Gray admonished. "No trash talk between teams. Play ball!"

Fluff snagged the ball and punted it at Brisa. But Brisa was busy admiring her pretty mane and missed the pass. The ball sailed across the field and landed right between the forelegs of—Andy!

"Here we go!" Kona cried, zipping toward the foal. "Up here, Andy. Pass me the ball. Pass it!!!!"

But Andy forgot all about Kona's coaching

and began bopping the ball around with his nose.

"Andy!!!!" Kona cried desperately.

"Oh, please, I'll pass you the ball if you'll be quiet about it," Thelma grumbled. She cantered up to her foal and kicked the ball away from him.

Of course, she didn't exactly watch where she was watching where she was

kicking, and the ball sailed straight to Sumatra, who began dribbling down the field for a goal.

"Noooooo!" Kona cried, zipping after her. Kona chased Sumatra so intently, in fact, that she might have bumped her nose into

Sumatra's flank. Sumatra lost control of the ball. But before Kona could scoop it up, Gray yelled out.

"Foul!" the squirrel called from down the field. *Crunch, crunch.*

Kona gaped down at Gray. He was squinting up at her between noisy bites of an apple.

"How can you referee and eat at the same time?" she demanded.

"I can do *anything* and eat at the same time," Gray declared.

"You're my kind of guy, Gray!" Sirocco said, winking at the squirrel.

"And the fouled player gets a penalty kick," Gray continued. "Go ahead, Sumatra. Place the ball in front of the other team's goal and give it a good wallop."

"But that's as good as giving her a goal!"

Kona protested.

"Maybe next time," Sumatra smirked, "you'll keep your nose to yourself."

Kona scowled at Sumatra.

"This isn't personal, Sumatra," Kona said. "It's just a game!"

"Of course," Sumatra said as she positioned her ball carefully before Kona's team's goal. Her kick sent the ball straight into the water trough, despite Kona's best efforts to block it.

"The score's now THREE to TWO," Gray announced.

"Grrr," Kona responded.

The rest of the game went like this: Sirocco kept drifting off to practice loop-de-loops. Thelma never tried to score: She only kicked the ball to amuse Andy.

And the other team was no better: Sumatra and Brisa started doing little dances with the ribbons of Sumatra's magic halo.

"Kick the ball, punt the ball, go team!" they cheered, before collapsing into giggles.

"You can't play soccer and be cheerleaders at the same time," Kona reprimanded them.

"Why not?" Brisa asked. "Gray can crack walnuts and referee at the same time."

Kona gasped and looked down at Gray. The squirrel was indeed knocking walnuts against the paddock fence, all while he made his referee calls.

Am I the only one who takes this game seriously? Kona complained to herself.

When it came to Andy, the answer was definitely yes. Try though she might, Kona just could not get the rambunctious colt to follow her coaching.

"No, no, Andy," she admonished him after

he kicked the ball in the wrong direction (for the fourth time). "Kick it this way!"

Or it was, "Andy, pass the ball. Don't try to score! Nooooo!" as Andy missed the goal by a mile.

Or, "Andy, if I've told you once, I've told you ten times, stop trying to fly and run for the ball."

And now Sumatra's team made another goal, and the score was tied three to three.

There are just a few minutes left to play. I've got to score, Kona told herself breathlessly. *If I don't, my team won't win!*

Aggressively, Kona scooped up the ball and kicked it to Sirocco. He passed it to Thelma, who nudged the ball toward Andy.

"Here you go, sweetie," she said. "Have fun."

"No, no," Kona protested, zipping down toward Andy.

"Pass the ball to me, Andy," she called to the foal. "Over here, little guy!"

Andy whinnied playfully at Kona, then nosed the ball down the field.

Down the field, Kona realized, in the wrong direction! Andy was moving the ball toward their own team's goal!

"No, no, Andy!" Kona called. Despite her best efforts, her voice was edgy now. "This a-way! Pass it to me!"

"*Wheeeee!*" Andy squealed with glee. He gave the ball a kick, sending it closer to the wrong goal, then trotted after it.

"Andddyyyyyy!" Kona neighed. She flew as fast as she could toward the ball, but the big foal was too quick for her. He pounced on the ball and gave it another resounding kick!

Klang!

"And the foal scores!" Benny announced as the ball clattered into the water trough.

Benny ruffled Andy's mane with his nose and said, "Thanks for the help, kid!"

"Goal!" Gray called as he munched on another walnut. "And the game goes to Sumatra, Brisa, Benny, and Fluff, FOUR to THREE!"

"*Andy!*"

Kona flapped her wings furiously, as she hovered before the foal's big, black eyes.

"Why didn't you do what I told you?" she reprimanded him. "You lost this game for us. I hope you're happy about it!"

But for the first time, perhaps ever, Andy didn't seem happy. He stared at Kona with wide, perplexed eyes. His lower lip trembled.

And that's when another angry voice rang out across the paddock.

"That's it!" Thelma bellowed, galloping over to cuddle Andy—and glare at Kona. "You're OUTTA here!"

"*Wah!*" Kona cried—and flew away from the paddock as fast as she could.

CHAPTER 5
A Solo Sport

Kona found refuge on a low-hanging tree branch in the middle of the dandelion meadow. She hid among the leaves and sniffled. Her halo of magical flowers sagged.

Part of Kona was ashamed of herself for yelling at Andy. But another part of her felt misunderstood!

"What's so wrong about wanting to win?" she murmured to herself tearfully. "I mean, isn't that the whole point of playing?"

"Kona."

Kona jumped as a voice rumbled up from

 66

beneath her. She used her front legs to part the leaves on her branch and peered downward.

It was Thelma! The mare was standing beneath the tree, gazing up at Kona with a mixture of irritation and compassion.

"Soccer is just a game," Thelma said. "Isn't that what you've been telling us?"

"Well, yes," Kona responded, fidgeting uncomfortably. "But I didn't say that winning the game doesn't matter! Didn't you want to beat them as much as I did?"

"You mean Sumatra, Brisa, Benny, and Fluff?" Thelma asked.

"Of course," Kona said. "It was us against them, in case you've forgotten."

"Actually, to me, Kona," the mare said, "it felt a lot like all of us . . . against you."

Shaking her head, Thelma loped away to graze next to Andy, Benny, and Fluff. Fluttering above them, Sirocco, Sumatra, and Brisa cast worried glances at Kona's tree, but gave Kona her space.

Feeling lonely, Kona sighed and looked around. She noticed an acorn resting on the end of her branch. With a shrug, she kicked the nut toward a knot in the tree's trunk.

Plunk. A hole in one!

But Kona just sighed. Scoring a direct hit wasn't fun without friends to share it with.

 68

And now that I think about it, she realized, *just playing with my friends is a lot more fun than beating them at a game.*

Kona snuck a glance at Sumatra, Brisa, and Sirocco. They were chasing each other through the air now, and giggling. They seemed happy.

Slowly and shyly, Kona flew over to her friends, wondering if they'd turn their flanks, tails, and cold shoulders on her.

But instead, the Wind Dancers gathered around her, their halos bright. Down on the ground, the big horses clustered together expectantly as well.

"I . . . want to be an 'us' again," Kona declared to her friends sheepishly. "And to forget about the 'them.' And . . ."

"Hey, Kona," Sumatra interrupted her.

Startled, Kona watched as Sumatra swooped down to the ground, scooped up a pinecone in her teeth, and tossed it toward her.

"Catch!" Sumatra yelled playfully.

Instinctively, Kona dashed for the pinecone and caught it in her teeth! With a laugh, she tossed it to Sirocco, who bopped it to Brisa.

But Brisa missed the pinecone. She was too busy admiring the magic gems in her halo! All the horses laughed—and none louder than Kona.

Sumatra flew closer to the violet filly and grinned at her.

"I kind of like playing catch, don't you?" she said. "No rules. No winning. No losing."

"Me, too!" Kona agreed, shooting Sumatra a grateful look. "I'm ready to say good-bye to soccer!"

"Oh, let's not do that!" Sumatra said, looking horrified. "I *like* soccer! We all do. It's just the crazy competitiveness that we don't like."

Once again, Kona felt embarrassment wash over her.

"But don't forget," Sumatra added kindly, "without you, we never would have started playing soccer. So we owe *you* a thank you."

"Really?" Kona said, looking hopefully at Brisa, Sirocco, and the big horses.

"Really," Sirocco agreed, swooping over for a nose nuzzle. Kona nuzzled him gratefully.

"So," Thelma said, now kicking the Jolly Ball off the ground and lobbing it up to Kona. "No more bullying your players, particularly my little foal?"

"No more!" Kona assured her, as she kicked the ball to Brisa.

"And no more gunning for every goal?" Brisa asked, as she knocked the ball back to Kona.

"Definitely not," Kona said with a laugh. This time, she kicked the ball to Sumatra. Sumatra caught it between her forelegs and looked at Kona hard.

"So how about for the next few days, we just kick the Jolly Ball around?" Sumatra asked. "No pressure. No points?"

All the horses held their breath. Would Kona be able to give up this part of the game?

"Deal!" Kona neighed happily.

"Yay!" Sumatra cried, tossing the ball down to Andy, who'd picked up a twig with his teeth and was waving it around. Accidentally, the foal knocked the ball with his stick and sent it sailing!

Kona watched the ball fly away, with a thoughtful smile—which quickly morphed into a sly grin.

"You know," she proposed to her friends with a twinkle in her eyes, "while we're taking our little break from competitive soccer, what do you say we try our hooves at baseball? I bet I could score more home runs than any of you!"

"KONA!" neighed every horse in the meadow.

"JUST KIDDING!" Kona giggled. Then she scooped another pinecone off the ground and gently tossed it to Andy. The little colt snapped the cone up in his teeth, then galloped away, whinnying mischievously with every step.

The Winner's Circle

The next day, Kona, Sumatra, Brisa, and Sirocco found themselves in a new game of soccer.

But this time they weren't playing. They were sitting on the edge of their seats (well, the edge of the schoolyard fence where they were invisibly perched) watching Leanna and her friends play another team on the field.

Kona's heart swooped with each kick, goal, and block, especially the ones made by Leanna.

But just like Sumatra, Brisa, and Sirocco, Kona cheered for *both* teams—right up until the whistle blew at the end of the game and the referee declared that Leanna's team had lost!

"Congratulations," Leanna said again and again, as she and her teammates high-fived the other team's players.

Kona looked at her fellow Wind Dancers guiltily.

"I guess I could have learned a thing or two more from Leanna," she said. "You know, about being a good sport."

"I think," Sumatra said, reaching out to give Kona a nose nuzzle, "you've learned now."

As the Wind Dancers fluttered up into the air and began flying back to their meadow, Kona peeked over her shoulder with a happy smile.

Sumatra was right.

After all, the trophies waiting for *both* soccer teams along the side of the field had been her idea.

And she was the one who had insisted that a trophy go to *every* player, no matter which team won.

Each tiny prize was made of an acorn cup filled to the brim with flowers from Kona's magic halo.

"After all," Kona said to her friends as they made their way home together, "everyone who knows *how* to play the game is a winner!"

Here's a sneak preview of *Wind Dancers* Book 6:

Horses Her Way

CHAPTER 1
Swim Team

*S*plash!

Two of the three fillies, Kona and Sumatra, were standing ankle-deep in the gentle water of a creek near their apple tree house.

Sirocco, on the other hand, was smack dab in the *middle* of the creek.

"SIR-OC-CO!" Kona and Sumatra neighed indignantly at their fellow Wind Dancer.

"What?" Sirocco said innocently as he joyfully thrashed in the water.

"This was *supposed* to be just a morning romp," Sumatra reprimanded the unruly colt.

"Right," Kona agreed. "To get our last taste of the creek before it gets too cold."

She glanced up at the tree branches hanging over the creek. The leaves were already turning golden yellow and russet red as autumn approached.

"So what's the problem?" Sirocco asked again.

Splash, splash, splash!

Now came a sweet sing-songy voice from the creek bank: "You're not romping, Sirocco! You're positively *wallowing* in the water!"

This was Brisa, curled up on a perfect little mound

of emerald moss. Her long, blonde mane shimmered. Her coral-pink coat gleamed. And her magic-halo jewels danced around her neck.

Sirocco rolled his eyes at the pretty little filly.

"I don't know why it matters to you, Brisa," he said. "You haven't come anywhere *near* the water."

"Of course not," Brisa said, widening her already huge eyes. "A damp mane? A matted tail? Hooves covered with creek silt? I don't think so."

Kona looked down a little sheepishly at the white socks on her forelegs. They were, indeed, mottled with mud.

Sumatra's pale green tail *did* look wet and stringy compared to Brisa's flowing blonde one.

And Sirocco was a complete mess!

But Sirocco didn't care if he was dirty!

And he didn't think his friends should, either.

"C'mon," he scoffed, using his nose to send a splash Kona's way. "It's our last dip of the season. Live a little!"

"*Eek!*" Brisa cried. She fluttered her wings hard and rose into the air. "You guys are going to get me all *dirty!*"

"Nobody here cares what you look like!" Sirocco bellowed.

"*I* care," Brisa said simply. And with that, she turned and began flying away.

Continue the magical adventures with Breyer's

Wind Dancers.

Let your imagination fly!

Sumatra

Sirocco

Kona

Brisa

Collect them all!

Visit www.BreyerHorses.com/winddancers for contests, games and fun!

Find these and other Breyer models, activity sets, games and more at your favorite toy store! Visit us online at **www.BreyerHorses.com** to get a free poster* and to register for online newsletters!